S0-AWT-744

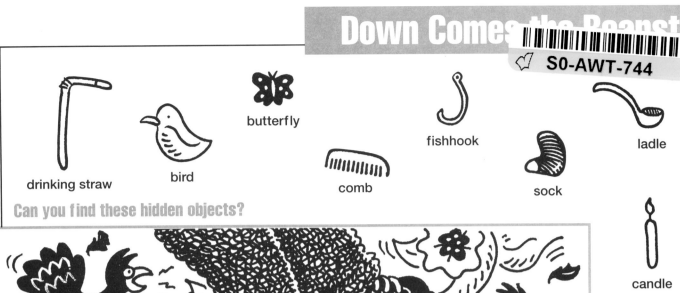

butterfly

bird

drinking straw

comb

fishhook

sock

ladle

Can you find these hidden objects?

candle

ring

heart

teacup

sea horse

clothespin

Illustrated by Ron Lieser

Highlights®

5

Wetlands Adventure

tack

candle

pencil

fork

fishhook

cane

golf club

ring

Can you find these hidden objects?

spoon

ice-cream bar

funnel

question mark

needle

crayon

heart

flag

i 50 F

pitcher

key

heart

egg

lollipop

fish

ring

pennant

Can you find these hidden objects?

fishhook

2 mushrooms

bat

button

arrow

teacup

trowel

ice-cream cone

Illustrated by Arieh Zeldich

Highlights®

1

mouse

fishhook

bowling pin

fish

spoon

carrot

banana

bell

teacup

penguin

wishbone

flashlight

eyeglasses

candle

trowel

knitted hat

boomerang

needle and thread

Can you find these hidden objects?

Illustrated by Chuck Dillon

Highlights®

Chickens Crossing

banana

candle

teardrop

envelope

arrow

hat

knitted hat

toothbrush

Can you find these hidden objects?

pliers

megaphone

heart

adhesive bandage

crescent moon

spool of thread

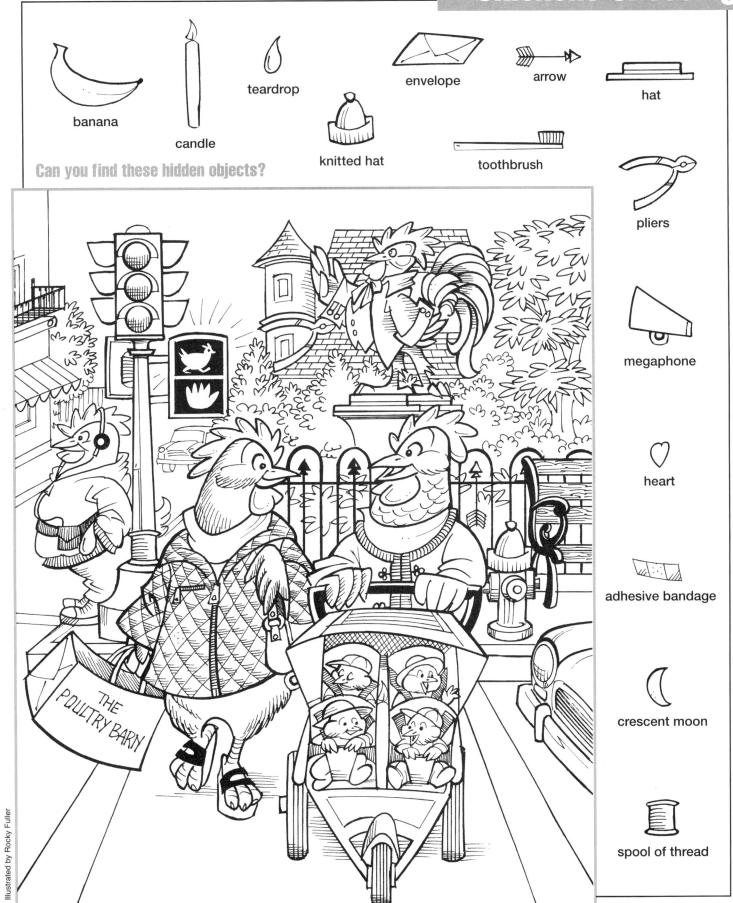

THE POULTRY BARN

Illustrated by Rocky Fuller

Highlights®

teacup

spoon

dog bone

comb

saltshaker

pencil

Can you find these hidden objects?

slice of pizza

snail

paper clip

flashlight

wishbone

fish

crescent moon

Illustrated by Maggie Swanson

Highlights®

ladder

pennant

nail

artist's brush

umbrella

glove

arrow

fan

crown

slice of pie

baby's rattle

wishbone

mask

Illustrated by Sally Springer

NO TRESPASSING ON THIS ISLAND!

Highlights®

Sliding Home

bell

candy cane

turtle

artist's brush

spatula

crescent moon

Illustrated by Maurie Jo Manning

Can you find these hidden objects?

bird

toothbrush

mitten

heart

muffin

teacup

spoon

Highlights®

Whose Turn?

mallet

banana

bell

toothbrush

candle

crescent moon

sock

safety pin

lollipop

pushpin

teacup

musical note

shovel

Can you find these hidden objects?

Illustrated by Charles Jordan

Highlights®

Maypole Dance

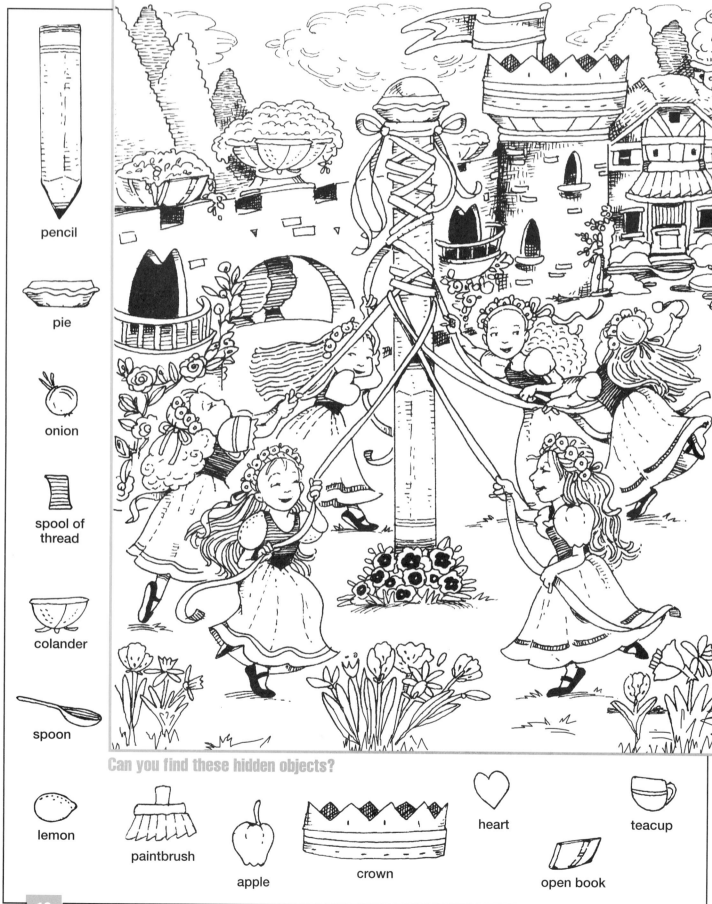

pencil

pie

onion

spool of thread

colander

spoon

Can you find these hidden objects?

lemon

paintbrush

apple

crown

heart

teacup

open book

Illustrated by Diana Zourelias

10

Highlights®

saucepan

shoe

crescent moon

fish

eyeglasses

ruler

lizard

ring

bell

nail

sailboat

spoon

ice-cream cone

horn

banana

Can you find these hidden objects?

PIZZA

Illustrated by Timothy Davis

Highlights®

Butterfly Watchers

doughnut

pencil

chef's hat

fried egg

walnut

apple

lollipop

envelope

boot

sailboat

grapes

necktie

spider

Can you find these hidden objects?

Illustrated by George Wildman

12

Highlights®

slice of cake

eyeglasses

candle

fishhook

mug

spoon

hammer

Can you find these hidden objects?

musical note

pencil

funnel

slice of bread

spatula

Illustrated by Charles Jordan

Highlights®

Happy the Hamster

tulip

cat

ice-cream cone

ring

sailboat

banana

Can you find these hidden objects?

tepee

pencil

shoe

feather

bird

fish

HAPPY

Illustrated by Susan T. Hall

14

Highlights®

toothbrush

worm

ice-cream bar

apple

leaf

trowel

mushroom

needle

crescent moon

pennant

feather

heart

tulip

ladle

sailboat

nail

ring

mug

mallet

boot

Can you find these hidden objects?

Illustrated by Olivia Cole

Highlights®

scissors

paper clip

shovel

spoon

pencil

ice-cream cone

Can you find these hidden objects?

T-shirt

banana

heart

fish

needle

candle

QRT 535

sailboat

bell

open book

paintbrush

hourglass

Illustrated by Timothy Davis

slice of pie

frying pan

boot

saw

toothbrush

flashlight

coat hanger

ring

Highlights®

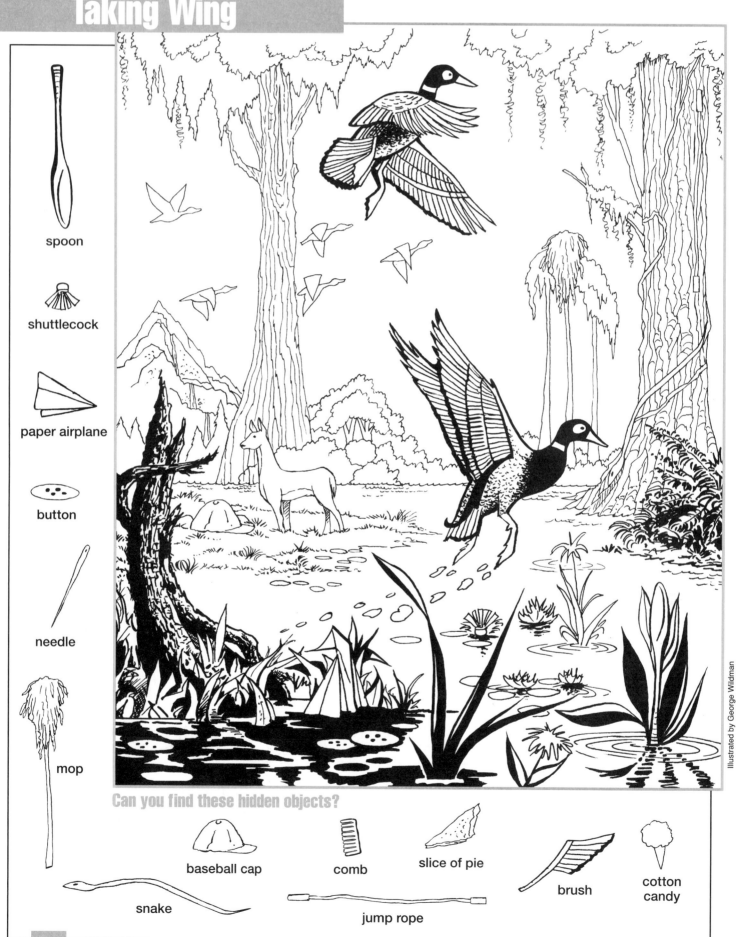

spoon

shuttlecock

paper airplane

button

needle

mop

Can you find these hidden objects?

baseball cap

comb

slice of pie

brush

cotton candy

snake

jump rope

Illustrated by George Wildman

Highlights®

Dad Flips a Burger

closed book

spoon

eyeglasses

cherry

ice-cream cone

hat

Can you find these hidden objects?

comb

pliers

pencil

banana

slice of lemon

candle

paper airplane

Illustrated by Ron Lieser

Highlights®

National Wildlife Week is April 21–29.

seashell

carrot

spoon

shoe

nail

cane

bowling pin

banana

Can you find these hidden objects?

light bulb

slice of pizza

drinking glass

rabbit

open book

toothbrush

pumpkin

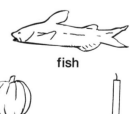

fish

candle

Illustrated by Jim Fitzgerald

Highlights®

Fire Safety Lesson

frying pan

slipper

fishhook

pear

pencil

banana

Can you find these hidden objects?

leaf

muffin

teapot

peanut

teacup

needle

bowl

FIRE DRILL TODAY

Illustrated by Maurie Jo Manning

Highlights®

December 8 is National Day of the Horse.

lemon

pencil

needle

nail

mushroom

ice-cream cone

pennant

Illustrated by Janet Robertson

Can you find these hidden objects?

fish

snake

mallet

hamburger

banana

candle

mouse

Highlights®

Setting Sail

drinking straw

envelope

toothbrush

baseball

golf club

tube of toothpaste

flag

comb

tack

spoon

snake

carrot

ice-cream cone

Can you find these hidden objects?

Illustrated by R. Michael Palan

Highlights®

23

A Family of Readers

bell

waffle

cane

oar

fishhook

domino

light bulb

pennant

mitten

TALES

Can you find these hidden objects?

airplane

heart

crescent moon

tack

pencil

stamp

hammer

comb

Illustrated by Arieh Zeldich

24

Highlights®

Paper towels were invented by Irvin and Clarence Scott in Philadelphia in 1907.

toothbrush

muffin

closed book

Can you find these hidden objects?

pliers

lollipop

crown

needle

comb

table

boot

trowel

fish

flag

sailboat

mallet

tack

nail

shoe

Illustrated by Olivia Cole

Highlights®

25

Trying Their Wings

comb

artist's brush

heart

sailboat

high-heeled shoe

glove

paper clip

Illustrated by Timothy Davis

Can you find these hidden objects?

banana

fish

toothbrush

ice-cream cone

bat

26

Highlights®

Botany Lesson

Can you find these hidden objects?

shoe
fish
heart
hatchet
crescent moon
bird
baseball
crown
sailboat
magnifying glass

tack
pencil
elf's hat
trowel
doughnut
slice of pie
feather
carrot
sock
candle
needle

Illustrated by Olivia Cole

Highlights®

National Pet Week is May 6–12.

candle

mitten

ring

crown

safety pin

window

football

handbell

pencil

artist's brush

scissors

muffin

needle

key

slice of lemon

doughnut

sock

Can you find these hidden objects?

OBEDIENCE SCHOOL

Illustrated by Jim Fitzgerald

Highlights®

Robert Frost, "America's Poet"

Can you find these hidden objects?

slice of pie
slice of pizza
toothbrush
fish
hammer
party horn
whale
clothespin
pencil
paintbrush
mug
sailboat
carrot
candle
mushroom
tack
crescent moon

The woods are lovely, dark and deep. But I have promises to keep And miles to go before I sleep...

Two roads diverged in a wood, and I— I took the one less traveled by.

R. FROST

PRESIDENT OF

Illustrated by Linda Weller

Water Slide

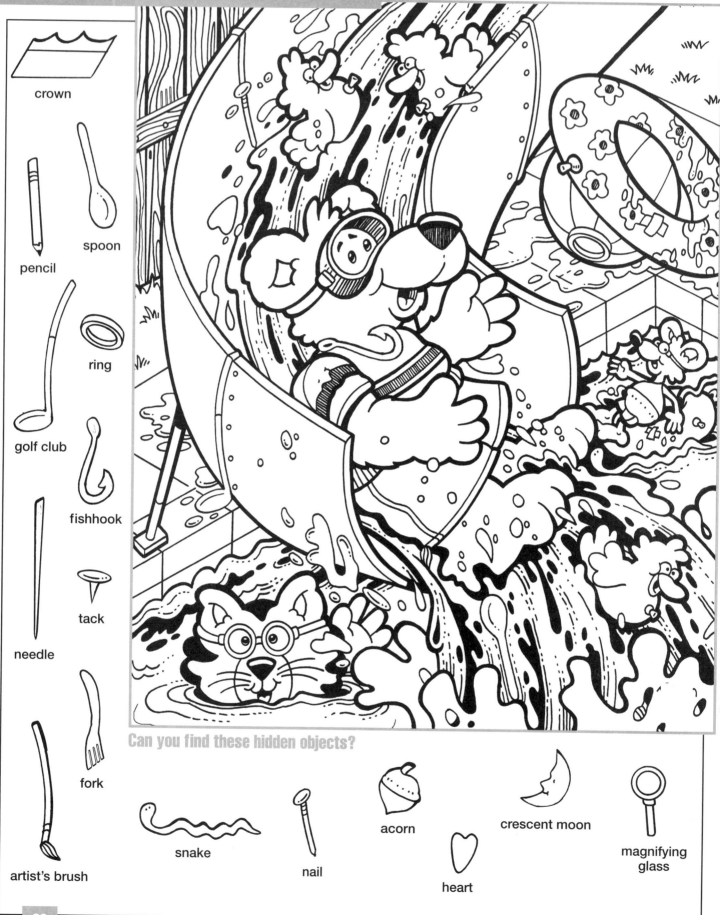

crown

pencil

spoon

ring

golf club

fishhook

needle

tack

fork

artist's brush

snake

nail

acorn

heart

crescent moon

magnifying glass

Can you find these hidden objects?

Illustrated by R. Michael Palan

Highlights®

high-heeled shoe

muffin

nutcracker

bird

ice-cream cone

slipper

crescent moon

Can you find these hidden objects?

drumstick

snail

button

saltshaker

ladder

pliers

flashlight

fish

canteen

Illustrated by Maurie Jo Manning

Highlights®

March is Youth Art Month.

slice of cake

pushpin

spatula

musical note

tack

golf club

magnifying glass

safety pin

ice-cream bar

sock

mitten

candle

Can you find these hidden objects?

Illustrated by Charles Jordan

Highlights®

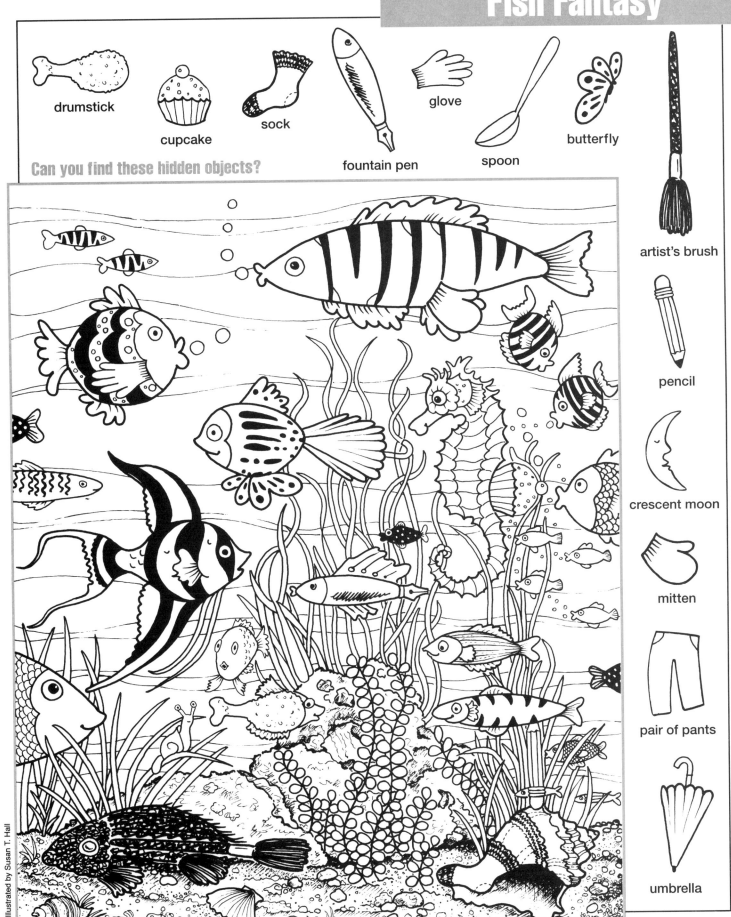

drumstick

cupcake

sock

fountain pen

glove

spoon

butterfly

Can you find these hidden objects?

artist's brush

pencil

crescent moon

mitten

pair of pants

umbrella

Illustrated by Susan T. Hall

Highlights®

May 23 is World Turtle Day.

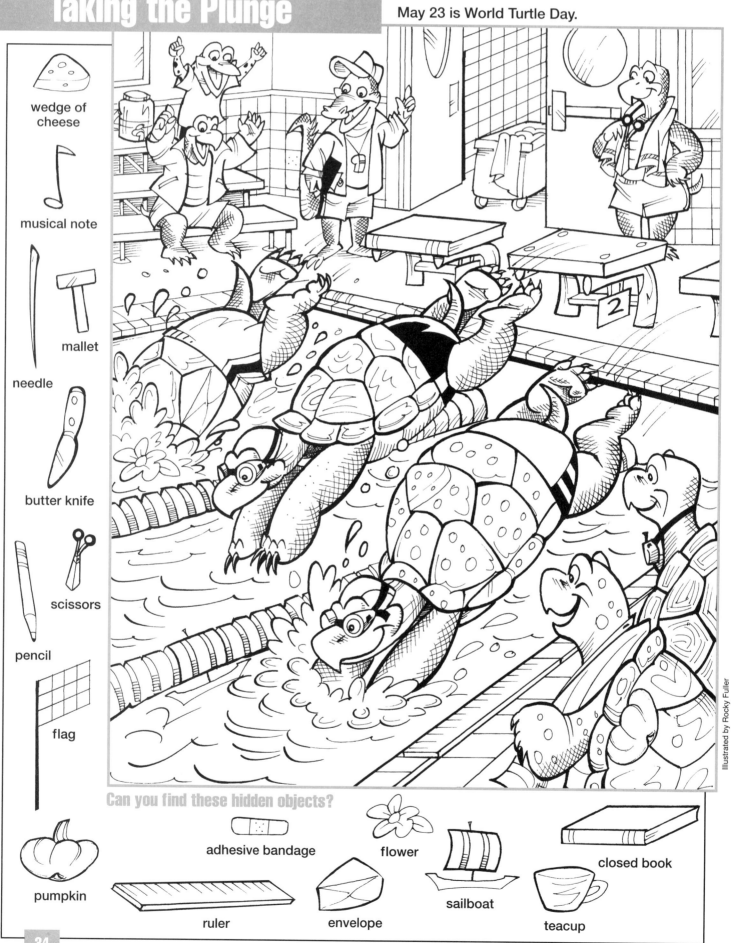

wedge of cheese

musical note

needle

mallet

butter knife

scissors

pencil

flag

Can you find these hidden objects?

pumpkin

ruler

adhesive bandage

envelope

flower

sailboat

teacup

closed book

Illustrated by Rocky Fuller

Highlights®

Malaysia gained independence from the United Kingdom on August 31, 1957— 50 years ago.

open book

slice of cake

heart

drinking glass

spaceship

toothbrush

Can you find these hidden objects?

boomerang

sailboat

knitted hat

snake

tack

comb

needle

trowel

Malaysia

MALAYSIA

SOUTH
CHINA
SEA

MALAYSIA

INDONESIA

Illustrated by Olivia Cole

Highlights®

Art Appreciation

mug

elephant's head

shoe

sailboat

artist's brush

golf club

crayon

teacup

candle

spoon

Can you find these hidden objects?

swan

dog

penguin

tube of toothpaste

megaphone

hammer

fish

crescent moon

acorn

sock

Illustrated by Linda Weller

36

Highlights®

ring

saucepan

tack

closed book

bicycle pump

Can you find these hidden objects?

pennant

fishhook

candle

carrot

slice of cake

pushpin

ice-cream bar

Illustrated by Charles Jordan

Highlights®

Dog's Delight

Fifty years ago, in 1957, the Wham-O company developed the first flying disk.

candle

fishhook

pencil

nail

crescent moon

clothespin

banana

pear

needle

slice of bread

ice-cream cone

wishbone

mushroom

feather

heart

arrow

Can you find these hidden objects?

Illustrated by Sally Springer

Highlights®

▼Page 1

▼Page 2

▼Page 3

THE POULTRY BARN

Highlights®

Answers

▼ Page 4

▼ Page 5

▼ Pages 6–7

Highlights®

▼Page 8

▼Page 9

▼Page 10

▼Page 11

Answers

▼ Page 12

▼ Page 13

▼ Page 14

▼ Page 15

Highlights®

▼Pages 16–17

▼Page 18

▼Page 19

Answers

▼Page 20

▼Page 21

FIRE DRILL TODAY

▼Page 22

▼Page 23

Highlights®

▼Page 24

▼Page 25

▼Page 26

▼Page 27

Highlights®

45

Answers

▼Page 28

▼Page 29

▼Page 30

▼Page 31

Highlights®

▼Page 32

▼Page 33

▼Page 34

▼Page 35

Answers

▼Page 36

▼Page 37

▼Page 38

▼Cover

Highlights®